## PRAISE FOR M

Tom Clancy fans open to a strong female lead will clamor for more.

— *DRONE*, PUBLISHERS WEEKLY

Superb! Miranda is utterly compelling!

— *BOOKLIST*, STARRED REVIEW

Miranda Chase continues to astound and charm.

— BARB M.

Escape Rating: A. Five Stars! OMG just start with *Drone* and be prepared for a fantastic binge-read!

— READING REALITY

The best military thriller I've read in a very long time. Love the female characters.

— *DRONE*, SHELDON MCARTHUR, FOUNDER OF THE MYSTERY BOOKSTORE, LA

A fabulous soaring thriller.

— *TAKE OVER AT MIDNIGHT,* MIDWEST BOOK
REVIEW

Meticulously researched, hard-hitting, and suspenseful.

— *PURE HEAT,* PUBLISHERS WEEKLY, STARRED
REVIEW

Expert technical details abound, as do realistic military missions with superb imagery that will have readers feeling as if they are right there in the midst and on the edges of their seats.

— *LIGHT UP THE NIGHT,* RT REVIEWS, 4 1/2
STARS

Buchman has catapulted his way to the top tier of my favorite authors.

— FRESH FICTION

Nonstop action that will keep readers on the edge of their seats.

— *TAKE OVER AT MIDNIGHT,* LIBRARY JOURNAL

M L. Buchman's ability to keep the reader right in the middle of the action is amazing.

— LONG AND SHORT REVIEWS

The only thing you'll ask yourself is, "When does the next one come out?"

— *WAIT UNTIL MIDNIGHT,* RT REVIEWS, 4 STARS

The first...of (a) stellar, long-running (military) romantic suspense series.

— *THE NIGHT IS MINE,* BOOKLIST, "THE 20 BEST ROMANTIC SUSPENSE NOVELS: MODERN MASTERPIECES"

I knew the books would be good, but I didn't realize how good.

— NIGHT STALKERS SERIES, KIRKUS REVIEWS

Buchman mixes adrenalin-spiking battles and brusque military jargon with a sensitive approach.

— PUBLISHERS WEEKLY

13 times "Top Pick of the Month"

# SOUTH POLE PEACHES AND CREAM

AN ANTARCTIC ICE FLIERS ROMANCE STORY

M. L. BUCHMAN

Buchman Bookworks

# Other works by M. L. Buchman: *(\* - also in audio)*

## Action-Adventure Thrillers

### Dead Chef
*One Chef!*
*Two Chef!*

### Miranda Chase
*Drone\**
*Thunderbolt\**
*Condor\**
*Ghostrider\**
*Raider\**
*Chinook\**
*Havoc\**
*White Top\**

## Romantic Suspense

### Delta Force
*Target Engaged\**
*Heart Strike\**
*Wild Justice\**
*Midnight Trust\**

### Firehawks
**MAIN FLIGHT**
*Pure Heat*
*Full Blaze*
*Hot Point\**
*Flash of Fire\**
*Wild Fire*
**SMOKEJUMPERS**
*Wildfire at Dawn\**
*Wildfire at Larch Creek\**
*Wildfire on the Skagit\**

### The Night Stalkers
**MAIN FLIGHT**
*The Night Is Mine*
*I Own the Dawn*
*Wait Until Dark*
*Take Over at Midnight*

*Light Up the Night*
*Bring On the Dusk*
*By Break of Day*
**AND THE NAVY**
*Christmas at Steel Beach*
*Christmas at Peleliu Cove*
**WHITE HOUSE HOLIDAY**
*Daniel's Christmas\**
*Frank's Independence Day\**
*Peter's Christmas\**
*Zachary's Christmas\**
*Roy's Independence Day\**
*Damien's Christmas\**
**5E**
*Target of the Heart*
*Target Lock on Love*
*Target of Mine*
*Target of One's Own*

### Shadow Force: Psi
*At the Slightest Sound\**
*At the Quietest Word\**
*At the Merest Glance\**
*At the Clearest Sensation\**

### White House Protection Force
*Off the Leash\**
*On Your Mark\**
*In the Weeds\**

## Contemporary Romance

### Eagle Cove
*Return to Eagle Cove*
*Recipe for Eagle Cove*
*Longing for Eagle Cove*
*Keepsake for Eagle Cove*

### Henderson's Ranch
*Nathan's Big Sky\**
*Big Sky, Loyal Heart\**
*Big Sky Dog Whisperer\**

## Other works by M. L. Buchman:

### Contemporary Romance (cont)

#### Love Abroad
*Heart of the Cotswolds: England*
*Path of Love: Cinque Terre, Italy*

#### Where Dreams
*Where Dreams are Born*
*Where Dreams Reside*
*Where Dreams Are of Christmas\**
*Where Dreams Unfold*
*Where Dreams Are Written*

### Science Fiction / Fantasy

#### Deities Anonymous
*Cookbook from Hell: Reheated*
*Saviors 101*

#### Single Titles
*The Nara Reaction*
*Monk's Maze*
*the Me and Elsie Chronicles*

### Non-Fiction

#### Strategies for Success
*Managing Your Inner Artist/Writer*
*Estate Planning for Authors\**
*Character Voice*
*Narrate and Record Your Own*
*Audiobook\**

## Short Story Series by M. L. Buchman:

### Romantic Suspense

#### Delta Force
*Th Delta Force Shooters*
*The Delta Force Warriors*

#### Firehawks
*The Firehawks Lookouts*
*The Firehawks Hotshots*
*The Firebirds*

#### The Night Stalkers
*The Night Stalkers 5D Stories*
*The Night Stalkers 5E Stories*
*The Night Stalkers CSAR*
*The Night Stalkers Wedding Stories*

#### US Coast Guard

#### White House Protection Force

### Contemporary Romance

#### Eagle Cove

#### Henderson's Ranch\*

#### Where Dreams

### Action-Adventure Thrillers

#### Dead Chef

#### Miranda Chase Origin Stories

### Science Fiction / Fantasy

#### Deities Anonymous

#### Other
*The Future Night Stalkers*
*Single Titles*

## ABOUT THIS TITLE

*Felisha Cole* has been living on 'The Ice' for the last four years. Memories of her life before Antarctica are stretching gossamer thin.

*Supply flights can reach the South Pole only three months a year. The New York Air National Guard flies in summer scientists, supplies, and the all-important fuel to run the generators that power the entire South Pole station.*

*Flight Engineer Steve Mason* hits The Ice for the first time as his unique, Hercules "Skibird" proves it can deliver to the coldest and most remote place on Earth.

*When the fading memory of her beloved Georgia peaches meet up with his Yankee sense of wonder, there's no predicting what their dreams can become together.*

# 1

## October

Felisha could *feel* it heading her way, like the first day of school after a sultry Georgia summer.

She'd trained herself for this, mentally refreshing old skills for a month. And for the last week she'd been flogging her small team through the procedures until they moved like a well-oiled machine.

It was her fifth full year on "The Ice" as those in the know called Antarctica. Two summers at Palmer out on the Peninsula, three full years at McMurdo, then she'd nailed the big ticket and spent the last two years at the South Pole.

Her pair of teammates could feel it, too, or they wouldn't be out here freezing their asses off along with her.

After a hundred and eighty-two days of darkness and beguiling twilight, the sun had risen at the Amundsen-Scott South Pole Station for the first time on September twenty-first. Only once in the following twenty-four hours had it dipped below the horizon before coming back to stay in the sky for the next hundred and eighty-two days.

But the South Pole, tucked so long in the deep freeze, didn't warm up quickly. It had taken over a month for the temperature to rise from a typical winter-day's minus seventy to today's spring-like minus forty-eight. It was finally balmy enough for the first plane to arrive from McMurdo Station.

"The first flight of the season," Hubert practically crowed.

"Freshies! Freshies! Freshies!" Lamar began to chant. She and Hubert picked up his chant, shouting louder and louder.

Clay, the skiway manager, was the only other one out in the cold, waiting to guide the flight to a stop on the taxiway. He picked it up too until they all broke up in laughter.

And her chest hurt from inhaling all of the freezing air despite her thick-knit peach scarf (all red and pink and orangey-yellow)—once a Georgia gal, always a Georgia gal.

The fat-cats at McMurdo had gotten their first load of freshie food, people, and supplies two full months ago—South Pole's turn now. There was going to be fresh fruit at dinner tonight!

The hydroponics provided salad greens winter 'round, which would have made the old timers whimper with delight. But she'd almost forgotten what a banana even looked like. And a peach, please let it be a sweet Georgia peach from home.

Except there wouldn't be. It was winter there now. She'd take a New Zealand peach. Except it was only spring there. Please let there be a peach.

"Tally-ho!" Lamar called out.

"Since when did you become a fox hunter?" Felisha sneered at him behind her scarf.

"A foremast hand. Since I became marooned on a sea of frozen ice. Like land-ho, only different."

"You're nineteen. You so aren't the ancient mariner, Lamar."

"A frozen sea at nine thousand three hundred feet." Hubert was always a little anal; a trait that served them well as a member of her fuel crew. He was actually an astrophysicist they'd borrowed from the IceCube neutrino detector, but down here everyone pitched in at everything. Especially with just thirty-nine winterovers during this year's nine months of inaccessibility.

Except under the most extreme medical emergencies, the Amundsen-Scott South Pole Station was unreachable from mid-February to late-October. It made preparing for the brief summer expansion to a hundred and fifty staff and scientists—plus visitors—more than a bit of a stress on the team.

She blinked hard behind her sunglasses—sunburn of the eyes was a major South Pole summer hazard—trying to sharpen her focus. She tried looking off to the side to catch sight of the black dot against the perfect blue sky with her peripheral vision.

All she saw was the furred edge of the hood of her Big Red parka.

By the time she turned back, it was visible straight on.

That put the plane near the outer marker that stood six and a half miles from the airfield. Meteorological personnel had dug that out of the winter snows. Flattening the winter's drifts and compacting the snow skiway had taken another two hundred people-hours. Then they'd staked flags every sixty meters down the whole twelve-thousand-foot length of the skiway because it was otherwise indistinguishable from the polar ice cap.

She'd helped the electricians extend the grid out to where the plane would stop. Once they'd dragged out three fuel tanks on sleds and a giant wheeled fire extinguisher bottle, they were finally ready. The Fire Team was warm inside the base unless something went sideways—though she was part of that crew too. The Unloading Team kept their vehicles warm in the garage until the last second.

For three long minutes the black dot crawled closer, changing to a black dot topped with the thin line of a hundred-and-thirty-foot wingspan and then to an LC-130H Hercules "Skibird" cargo plane of the Air National Guard's 109th Airlift Wing.

The wind was sweeping in its usual direction—out of the eastern hemisphere into the western—though slow today at under twenty knots. Here, two hundred meters from the South Pole, every direction was north except one, so they had to use hemispheres for direction. Actually, they used sectors. The wind consistently blew from the eastern Clean Air Sector, which was a no-fly, no-drive zone so that sensors could measure the particulates and global pollution accurately. The Skibird was arriving up the Downwind Sector.

What all that meant was that they couldn't hear the massive plane until the big skis which hung around the wheels were actually down on the snow, because the sound was being blown away.

Then it began carefully reversing its engines. Like landing on an ice-skating rink, the least error could send the aircraft skidding sideways. Sliding off the groomed skiway here wasn't like sliding off a paved runway onto the grassy median. Here the plowed-up snowbanks were likely to rip off the landing gear or completely destroy the plane if the pilot didn't nail the landing.

But even though it was the first run of the season, the pilot hit it dead clean.

The first of seventy-six supply flights scheduled this summer from McMurdo was finally here. They damn well better not have swiped *her* peaches out of the freshies box. If there were any.

## 2
_____

THERE'D BEEN WEEKS OF EXTRA TRAINING NEEDED TO become a Skibird Flight Engineer after he was fully qualified on the C-130 Hercules aircraft. Operating on polar ice, the 109th's specialty, required many skills no other birds had to worry about. Lubricant freezing, reheating a super-chilled plane, even a three day "Kool School" training for survival skills on the Greenland ice cap in case they were forced down.

The main goal was being down in the cold for as few minutes as possible. Land, unload, reload, and get the hell out of Dodge. That had been drilled endlessly into his head—like the cold was some monster—until he felt a chill of nerves even landing at the South Pole.

They'd departed their home base during a particularly nippy New York fall and flown down to McMurdo Station through Christchurch, New

Zealand. For two weeks they'd been flogging loads out of McMurdo to help reopen various summer camps.

Sergeant Steve Mason thought he was ready for the slap of cold.

Not even close.

One second he was standing inside a nice warm Hercules cargo bay wondering why he was wearing so damn many clothes. The seven layers of the Gen III Level 7 ECWCS—Extended Cold Weather Clothing System was utterly ridiculous and he felt like the Stay-Puft marshmallow man. Substituting the fleece jacket with the Christmas sweater Mom had knit and sent early because he'd be deployed down here on The Ice for the October to February resupply runs, only meant that he couldn't unzip it for comfort.

Behind him the center of the bay was filled with six pallets of supplies and twenty personnel who'd been crammed into the fold-down side seats for three hours.

In front of him the rear ramp cracked open…and the heat rushed out of the plane faster than smoke up a chimney. The cold slapped his chest straight through Mom's sweater and the two layers of long johns. He scrambled to zip up his wind shell, jacket, light parka, and finally his heavy parka. His ECWCS was rated to minus sixty—and his plane to only minus fifty—but he could still feel the cold clawing for a way in on both of them.

Jansen was laughing at him.

"It's my first year on The Ice, give me a break."

"FINGY!"

*Aw crap!* He kept it to himself. He'd be the "Fucking New Guy" for at least the entire season but griping about it would only make him *more* of a target. However, he'd picked up chunks of the Antarctic parlance during his first two weeks here. "You ain't no OAE yourself, Jansen."

"Second summer. I'll always be one closer than you, Steve."

"Close don't count." And he knew that. Old Antarctic Explorer status meant that you had lived and worked on The Ice for a lot of summers—or been crazy enough to winterover. Word was that the hardcores only counted it if you did your winter at the South Pole. Minus fifty...*in the spring!*

"Yeah. Yeah. Yeah. Time's wasting. Get a move on."

The ramp wasn't even on the snow yet, but he hustled along it so that he reached the snow the same moment it did. This wasn't like McMurdo where you could power down the engines and hang out while the unload happened. In fact, it was about the only time anywhere that the big propellors were left spinning during load or unload operations.

The plane's engines were idled, but not shut down. Turned off, they could chill in thirty minutes and freeze hard in an hour.

The rule was two hours max on the ground, not even enough time to look around much.

At the end of the ramp, he was nearly trampled. A

team of six people hurried aboard to start the unload just as the excited crowd of science FINGYs were rushing down behind him. That whole mess was Loadmaster Jansen's problem.

His problem was—already waiting at the fuel taps under the wing.

The two-thousand-mile round trip from McMurdo to the Pole used all the fuel a standard C-130 could carry and still have a generous reserve. But the LC-130H—the special conversion for polar work—had a pair of extended range tanks that carried twenty-five hundred gallons on top of the reserves. The South Pole Station siphoned that off from every flight to the pole to run their power generators.

They had already run a yellow six-inch hose to the plane from a cluster of four-foot-diameter tanks laying on sledges in the snow like steel sausages. A drip pan had been shoved under each connection in the hose to catch even the smallest leak. Spills of even a drop on the pristine snow weren't allowed. He'd had more than a few lectures on that and the mounds of paperwork required if any was spilled.

Though he couldn't see inside their raised hoods, all three people of the ground team were clearly awaiting his laggard arrival.

The fuelies here were ready to rock and roll, not giving him an instant to take in the view.

"I heard winterovers had dropped down a gear and

were moving slow by the time spring arrived," he greeted them.

"Sun rose over a month ago. Spring has come and gone. This is high summer."

"At minus forty-eight." He opened the service port and checked the settings to make sure nothing was set to flow until the hose was hooked up.

"Downright balmy. Y'all are the ones who don't operate below minus fifty. We're the ones who had to carve out your sub-zero skiway these last few weeks down in the sixties. Come back at Christmas, we'll hit the minus teens by then. That's fine times."

He tried to see the speaker's face. All he could see was hood, sunglasses, and scarf with a giant peach centered over her mouth and nose—Mom would like the colorwork of the knit picture, it actually looked like a giant peach—but it couldn't hide the deeply Southern female voice. He hadn't expected a woman, mostly because he'd been told they were rare on The Ice and he'd figured that meant scientist, not fuelie.

"He's staring," one of the other two spoke for the first time. He had the out-West cowboy sort of tone.

"Shallow as a toad in a hole. Shee-it! A New York Neanderthal. A round of applause for another airman from the New York Air National Guard 109th Airlift Wing." The crew applauded with a soft slapping of gloves.

"New York and proud of it," he bowed to each of

them. Then he knocked loose the pipe cap that led to the plane's fuel tanks.

She mounted her hose to his plane so fast that he barely saved his glove-covered fingers from getting jacked into the connection.

He checked, but she'd done it clean. "You ready?"

"Hello. Standing here. Lamar, go keep an eye on the tanks. Hubert, walk the line and check for leaks. Remember, cold makes leaks."

"Never give up! Never surrender!" They both thumped their fists to their chest then raised it just above their shoulders to the side.

"Klingon?" He asked as they'd hurried off. Not that he had a clue about that sort of thing. Steve kept an eye on the two men, but they followed the hose line which had been laid well clear of the propellors.

"Oh, FINGY. You're so sad," the woman shook her head enough to shift the big hood, but she didn't explain why. "You gonna hit it or do I have to? I thought you boys got nervous sitting on the ground for a second longer than you had to."

Steve hit the feed and the hose stiffened as it filled with AN8 fuel. "Twenty-five hundred gallons of prime fuel. This ought to last you for a bit."

"Fifty-nine hours," her tone was definitely laughing at him.

"Excuse me?"

"No excuse for a FINGY."

Steve sighed. His tour flying around The Ice might

only last until February, but it was looking to be a long summer.

"But if you behave, we might forgive you. We burn roughly four hundred thousand gallons a year to run the station. We tinker with solar, but it's dark half the year. Wind turbines hate frequent hundred-knot winds at temperatures forty degrees below where their lubricants freeze. All our power comes from burning this jet fuel. Which includes heat, cooking, labs, moving telescopes, lights, computers, fuel for the small planes that can only carry fuel one way so they need a refill to go away again, and suchlike. Oh, and the snow compacters that built your little skiway, too. We keep an extra two hundred thousand in the tanks as a reserve."

"How many folks are down here?" He kept an eye on the gauge, but it was his first chance to look around.

From the air, they were on a white plain flatter than the one time he'd driven across the Midwest states. Down here on the ground there were drifts and hummocks around every single structure, as if the snow was offended by each man-made intrusion. There were several small structures that protruded from the snow like the fins of some underground behemoth. What looked like the front of two oversized Quonset huts disappeared into the ground...snow.

There was only one structure in the area that rose more than a single story—the main building. He could see a couple more smaller structures a kilometer...to the north? From here, just about everything was "to the north."

The Pole Station was the only structure that wasn't sitting on the snow. It looked like a broad, two-story, blue-steel industrial building—perched aloft on massive stilts.

"Thirty-nine folks this winter. One-fifty for the summer," she answered his question after giving him the time to scan the area.

"Huh."

"Huh?" she responded.

"Best I've got."

"You're a strange and nameless man, FINGY."

"Steve. Sergeant Steve Mason. You got one?"

"Felisha. Well, Brick—think I'll call you Brick—"

"Thick as?"

She began humming the refrain from Jethro Tull's *Thick as a Brick* album.

"I was afraid of that. I'm just trying to decide if being called Brick is better than Fucking New Guy. Maybe."

She laughed. Felisha had a great laugh. "First question most folks ask is where's the South Pole."

"Based on the name of the station, I'm sure it's somewhere hereabouts. But there's probably some barely survivable weird initiation right before it can be revealed. I figured it was safer not to ask."

"Got it in one." She waved a gloved hand toward the station. "At solar midnight, which lasts us some three fine months down here, you wait for the temperature to reach minus a hundred. It might do that more than occasionally. You come out of a two-hundred-degree sauna in nothing but your sneakers and sprint off to the Pole marker and back. Called the Three Hundred Club. Then you really know where the South Pole is down to your bones."

"Down to your *frozen* bones."

Again that great laugh.

To keep her near, he told stories about the antics of his nieces and nephew. The four of them *were* downright hilarious. But the twenty-five hundred gallons was offloaded far too soon.

He could only watch as the crew rolled up hoses, collected drip pans, and hooked up a tracked snow cat to tow the fuel sleds toward one of the buried Quonset huts.

Felisha waved, "Next time, Brick."

He waved back. He didn't ask "Next time what?" But he was actually looking forward to finding out.

He climbed aboard with the tens of thousands of pounds of recycling and garbage that they'd be hauling back to McMurdo. From fuel and freshies to garbage scow.

## 3

THE 109TH AIRLIFT WING HAD THREE LC-130H Hercules working the McMurdo-South Pole shuttle, so it was a week before she met Brick again under the airplane wing.

Felisha had enjoyed bantering with him. After an entire nine-month winter being shut in together, the station crew knew all of each other's wisecracks. Being one of the three women, she knew them far better than most. The newbies who'd been filtering south were... exhausting to be around. They were too much on the hustle—trying to cram an entire lifetime's opportunity into three months.

"Four *years?*" Steve Mason shouted loudly enough for Lamar and the summer temp to be twisting to look toward them from the filling fuel tanks. They'd lost Hubert back to his IceCube neutrino detector when he'd gotten two assistants of his own to manage. They really only needed him for the crossover season from winter to summer and back.

She shrugged. Four years she'd been on The Ice year-round, and she could feel her connection to the rest of the world stretching thinner and thinner. A thread so fine it might snap and she'd never notice. Would she wake up twenty years from now as the Ice Queen and wonder what the hell had happened? Or would she count it as years well spent? Damned if she knew.

"And you haven't been back to the States in all that time?" Brick was still aghast.

"Oh, let's see. Half-day flight to McMurdo. Another full day to Christchurch. Day and a half to the States with another half-plus to Georgia: call it three full days of travel. And I lose a half day to time zones, but I gain it back on the return, so we won't count that."

His sunglasses hid if his eyes were crossed yet.

"Except, oh wait, I'd be flying most of that Space-A and you know how much extra available space you guys have on a typical flight. And, oopsie, shitty weather at McMurdo or here grounds you for a week. So, a two-week vacation—during the busy summer season, mind, when I'm needed most—gets me less than a handful of days on the ground in Georgia. During *their* winter because flights only reach the pole in the middle of the Georgia winter. Not quite the deluxe vacation I'd be looking for."

"Well...shee-it!" The Southern pronunciation in his Yankee accent was enough to make her laugh.

"I do miss peaches though. My Mama lived in Clarkesville, Georgia."

"Yeah, I noticed your scarf. Good peach country?"

"The best. The North Georgia Mountains, that's the south end of the Blue Ridge to a Yankee, wrap as close around Clarkesville as Mama's hug. Amazing country."

"Big place?" Brick sat on the foot-thick snow ski, leaving her to watch the gauges. She'd give him about thirty seconds before the cold conducted right through his suit.

"Seventeen hundred."

"Beats me. Wheelerville, New York, which snuggles up against the Adirondacks cracks a thousand on a busy day. Born and raised there. We— Yikes!" He launched to his feet and started rubbing his ass.

He was like a one-man comedy show. "Let me guess, you still sleep in your old bedroom when you go a-visitin'."

"Every chance I get. Mom makes the best apple pie there is."

And Felisha could feel the light going out despite the sun sparkling off the snow.

Five years since she'd tasted Mama's peach cobbler. The cancer had already been Stage Four when the docs found it. And like the stoic single mom she was, she hadn't said a word while Felisha was doing her second summer on The Ice at Palmer. She'd made it back just in time to watch Mama die.

She did her best to put it aside, but it took most of the fun out of the day.

**4**

———————

IT TOOK THE REST OF THEIR TIME UNFUELING, BUT STEVE finally coaxed the story out of her, then was sorry that he had. His mom was still so full of life that he felt guilty. She was the school principal for the hundred and twenty K-8 students in their small town.

Felisha hadn't ever known her father. A summer fling with an itinerant peach picker.

His own dad was a long-term state representative—never farther away than the state capital in Albany, he could commute home most nights. As the 109th Airlift Wing's base in Schenectady was between Albany and Wheelerville, he and Dad often got together for breakfast.

It sounded as if Felisha had no one except The Ice. He couldn't imagine what that was like.

No quiet sunrises out fishing on Caroga Lake with

Dad. No weekend barbeques with his two sisters showing up with their families.

"Why do you stay?" The moment he asked it, he was sorry. *Because she had no place to go back to, idiot.*

She was silent through the whole shutdown and disconnect process.

Rather than waving goodbye from the snowcat hauling the fuel tanks, she wandered back over to the plane as her team drove toward the fuel arch.

This time he kept his mouth shut. He wished he could see her face, but that wasn't going to happen. Today *was* warmer than his first trip to the pole, by five whole degrees to minus forty-three.

"Hey Brick. Do me a favor? Don't spread that around. I left my past behind and swore I was only going to look ahead. I loved Mama, but she wouldn't want me wallowing in it."

"And you're not doing that here?"

Her silence said he still hadn't learned when to keep his mouth shut. She slowly turned a three-sixty as if scanning the whole horizon for an answer.

"Sorry."

"No. It's okay. It's a question I've been asking myself a lot lately. Have a safe flight." And she walked away.

## 5

Four hours later, Brick's LC-130H was unexpectedly back and they were reversing the process —dragging out transport tanks and refilling the wing tanks.

"Easy come, easy go," Felisha said as they pumped every drop of the twenty-five hundred gallons they'd unloaded this morning back into the plane's tanks.

"Storm slammed into McMurdo with no warning when we were just an hour out. Had to tap nearly the whole reserve getting back here."

"Better than landing on untested snow out in the wild white yonder," Felisha pointed out at the empty white plain. "Eight kinds of nasty if you'd had to do that. Soft snow, three-meter-high sastrugi drifts that would rip off your gear, and crevasses are just a few of the fun features we offer here on The Ice."

"Ones I'd probably rather not know about."

"Depends, some of them are fun. Though there is a regrettable lack of decent pubs."

Brick laughed at her joke which was nice, "I heard the closest one is the Ukrainians' out on the peninsula."

"Vernadsky. Fifteen hundred nautical, half a continent that way," she pointed perpendicularly to the runway.

They were rolling up the hoses, they had enough fuel now in the Hercules for another attempt at McMurdo—after the storm there passed.

Her crew did the chest thump salute—*Never give up. Never surrender*—before driving the equipment back toward the garage arch.

When he asked about that again, she decided to leave him guessing.

Instead she offered, "You're here for at least a day. Would you like the nickel tour?"

He made a show of slapping his pockets, which were inaccessible under his multiple parkas. "Can I owe you?"

"Sure, I'll trust you, Brick, but just this one time. You'll owe me." Felisha smiled at the words as they came out of her own mouth. Steve Mason had been really decent as she'd spilled her guts out on the snow. She'd been worrying about his reaction since the moment his plane had departed, twice as much when she heard it was returning. But he'd treated her no differently on his return. Damned decent of him.

Her first full year on The Ice, she'd made the mistake of talking about Mama's death. It had turned into a pity party so thick she couldn't seem to ever climb out of it. People were so careful around her that it felt as if they weren't even being human. Her best solution had been work and then shutting herself in her room. It had made for a long, lonely winter that first year.

Brick didn't do that.

She led him into the fuel arch, arriving just as the snowcat had finished towing the now empty transport tanks back inside.

"Holy shit!"

The fuel arch was the single biggest structure at the South Pole other than the sixty-five thousand square feet of the station building itself. Though it didn't look it. Most of its width and its entire length were packed tightly with large tubular, white tanks of fuel laid horizontally in stacks of five. Many of the surfaces were shrouded with hoar-frost ice.

Brick's shock was a common reaction. She knew the next five questions and saved him the trouble.

"Thirty, twenty-thousand-gallon tanks. Six hundred-thousand-gallon capacity. Ambient temperature of minus sixty. You know that AN-8 fuel gels at minus seventy-six Fahrenheit, so there's no vapor pressure to worry about. The fuel is very stable at this temperature."

"Never thought that through."

"I wouldn't go throwing around a lighter, but you probably could. It's as stable as most any liquid here in the big chiller."

He was nodding, "Where next?"

"Your Yankee hustle is showing. You're grounded for at least twenty-four hours."

"Caught," he shrugged it off as he laughed. It was a good sound inside the steel arch. "So...*where next?*" He said it like a high-voiced school boy and she returned his laugh. Not many did that to her. She wasn't some sour cynic, but when had she forgotten about laughing?

She led him down the length of the tunnel.

At the mid-point, she led him up an icy spiral stairway that climbed two stories to the surface. "Emergency exit. Of course, if things go that wrong, we're screwed and probably wouldn't make it out."

"Don't you have backups?"

"Yes, we have a six-month supply stash in a remote tunnel, but I wouldn't want to be counting on it. We need a thousand gallons of fuel a day for normal winter operation, roughly double that in summer. We lose the fuel in this arch and we're screwed. Think dehydrated food, minimal water, no showers, heat in just one or two spaces. Not pretty."

"Wow! What's it been like living out on the edge like this for two years?"

She glanced in his direction as she forced open the

door. FINGYs didn't tend to ask a tough question like that.

Once they were out, she made a note that her team had go get up here with shovels soon. The snow was drifting around the head of the stairwell again.

"Some folks ride high on the adrenaline of it. Others get creeped out and bail on their winter contract when the very last flight is loading and it's too late to replace their sorry behinds. I always just took it in stride. Turning from Monroe Street onto Water to get a take-out pizza or hustling down Interstate 85 into Atlanta, I'm far safer here."

"You're an alarmingly sensible person."

"Shush! That's a secret."

"Yes, ma'am."

"Here's another one." She pointed.

## 6

STEVE COULD FEEL HIS JAW DROP AND THERE WASN'T A thing he could do about it.

He was here.

A large blue-printed sign stated this was the geographical South Pole. The two contrasting quotes printed on it stated just how different this place could be for different people.

There was Amundsen's quote to one side:

*December 14, 1911*

*So we arrived and were able to plant our flag at the geographical South Pole.*

And Scott's heartbreaking one to the other:

*January 17, 1912*

*The Pole. Yes, but under very different circumstances from those expected.*

In front of the sign, a metal pipe stuck up out of the snow. Atop it was a lovely bright-brass marker in the shape of a compass. It was inscribed with January 1 of the prior year, "National Science Foundation," and "Geographic South Pole, Latitude 90° South."

"Wow. That really brings it home, doesn't it?" He ran a hand down the shaft inscribed with names.

Felisha pointed at her own. "It's all the winterovers from last year. We have a design contest in mid-winter and then the shop guys fabricate it—nobody gets to see it once it's done. This year's will be planted and unveiled January 1st. The old ones are all in a display case inside the base."

Her name here, before January 1st, meant that she'd winterovered the year before.

"And this January 1st, you'll be on this year's?"

"You'll be able to see for yourself."

"Yes, but will your name be on next year's?"

Felisha didn't stiffen or turn away, instead she changed like someone had thrown a light switch. Suddenly hard and aggressive, she shoved his chest. With so much padding, he barely felt the impact as he tumbled to the snow.

"What?" Remembering how cold his butt got sitting on the Hercules ski, he scrambled to his feet.

"What is it with you and the questions?"

"Am I supposed to have a clue what you're talking about?"

She turned her back on him and walked away.

Steve wasn't sure if he was supposed to follow her. Usually, like with his sisters, he knew exactly what he'd done—he'd often spent time planning it. They had been two against one growing up and he'd had to be sneaky. This time he had no idea. But, as she wasn't walking back toward the station, he decided it was safe to follow. Maybe the tour was still on?

Their destination quickly became clear. Most of a football field away was a circle of flags. He'd read about this. It was every flag of the Antarctica Treaty nations in a semi-circle around the ceremonial South Pole, squarely in front of the Amundsen-Scott South Pole Station.

The ice here was moving toward the sea at ten meters a year. When they'd built the station, this had been the geographical South Pole. It was strange to think of something as impossibly enormous as the polar plateau, thousands of miles across and over a mile thick, being in motion. He looked over his shoulder at this year's true geographical pole marker. Yet the plateau moved. So permanent and so ephemeral at the same time.

Felisha was staring at the ceremonial marker. A waist-high barber pole topped with a reflective metal sphere.

He stepped up a quarter turn from her and looked down at his own reflection. Anonymous in his heavy green parka. By contrast, she shone in the Big Red one of the US Antarctic Program.

He tried to remember the boy growing up in Wheelerville. He'd spent a lot of his youth skiing; the

Adirondacks were right out their back door after all. He'd had dreams of the Olympics or being one of those ski school guys who had his pick of the ski bunnies.

Instead he was standing at the South Pole with an Air National Guard 109th Airlift Wing patch on his arm. He liked this guy, but couldn't make sense that this was somehow him.

He glanced over at the unmoving Felisha, "What do you see when you look at your reflection?"

"Got a camera? I'll take your photo for you. Everyone wants their photo taken here." She didn't turn toward him. But her voice was more dead than alive.

"Felisha. What did I say to piss you off so much?"

"Nothing." Even the charming Southern gloss had been stamped out of it.

He folded his arms over his chest. "Okay then, what did *you* say to piss yourself off so much?"

That got him a movement that might have included a half smile. "Way too many things."

"Help to share any of them?"

"What, the story of my life wasn't enough?"

"Your mother died and you moved to Antarctica for four straight years. You are now officially an Old Antarctic Explorer past anyone arguing, so that means you are totally fearless. But your 'life's story'? Christ, I don't even know your last name."

She still didn't look up for a long time.

When she finally spoke, her words were so irrelevant that they made almost no sense at all.

"That way," she pointed in the direction they'd been walking to reach this marker, "past the skiway is the Dark Sector. It has the IceCube neutrino detector buried a mile down into the ice. You can see the telescope about a kilometer ahead. To the right is the Clean Air Sector. A hundred and thirty-degree no-go zone because we're measuring global air quality. Behind us is the Quiet Sector. There's a major seismographic station about ten klicks that way. And the way you came in is the Downwind Sector. It's the way you'll depart as well. We—"

"Jesus, Felisha! You could have just said you didn't want to talk." Steve turned and headed for the station building.

## 7

Felisha watched him walk halfway to the station before she snapped out of whatever weird headspace she'd slid into.

"No. Wait."

He kept going.

"Brick!"

Nothing.

"Steve!"

That stopped him.

She hurried over. "I'm sorry. I just—"

He waited her out.

"I've spent a long time never talking about myself more than I have to."

"Then why did you choose *me* to dump your 'life story' on?"

"I—" she looked around. Nothing but white snow and the blue station. The gray airplane with its red tailfin was parked on the other side of the building. "I have no idea."

His stance softened but he still didn't speak.

"Four years," she felt a shudder that had nothing to do with the cold. "It's a long time to have no home. Mama never owned a place. I couldn't even afford community college. I was working full-time from the day I turned sixteen. Earned my commercial driver's license at eighteen. Started with home fuel oil deliveries. Got into fueling planes when I was twenty. I was never a beaker, a scientist, always just a support grunt and I've loved it. Sweet Jesus on white toast, this is all coming out jumbled up."

"Smart woman who figured out how to do something most people can't even imagine." He waved a hand in a sweep that seemed to encompass all of The Ice. "You're on a roll, Felisha. Don't stop now."

She glanced back at the metal sphere of the South Pole marker.

"Something spooking you?"

All she could do was nod.

"Wondering how you became the person reflected in that little globe?"

Again she managed a nod as she turned back to stare at him. Had she been that obvious?

"Yeah, I got that feeling myself there. I'm guessing that you don't like what you saw?"

No, that wasn't it. "It's more as if I don't recognize her."

"Because she's in Antarctica? Being here is what's surprising the daylights out of me."

"Lot of volume to surprise out, daylight lasts six months here."

"Helpful," Steve teased her.

Much to her own surprise, she managed a laugh. "Ever since you landed I've been wondering what I'm doing. After four years gone, Georgia seems like a strange and semi-mythical place. As if I was barely half-connected anymore to where I lived all of my natural-born life other than Antarctica. But if I leave The Ice, then what? I don't have a home or any folk to go back to. You talk about your Mom's apple pie, breakfast with your dad, sisters, nieces...This girl doesn't have none of that pulling me back. But here for another year? Another twenty? I don't know. I just don't know."

"Shit, Felisha, all I really wanted was your last name."

The laugh just burst out of her.

She was glad for the hood, sunglasses, and wooly scarf that kept Steve from seeing the tears that came with it.

## 8

"HOLY SHIT!"

"What?"

Steve could only shake his head and stare. They were only about three steps past the inner door of the "airlock" entry into the South Pole station.

Felisha had thrown back the hood of her Big Red and then shrugged it off before jamming the thick peach scarf into one of its sleeves.

"You're not what I was...expecting." All he'd ever seen of her was the scarf and sunglasses buried inside a deep-furred hood. Layers of gloves and insulating layers meant that he hadn't seen so much as a wrist. He'd built half a hundred images in his head, many of them Southern-belle blonde, some darkly African-American, some just plain-Jane but why would he really care. He liked her. But none of them had been even close.

"And what weren't you expecting?" She was glaring at him with a fist on one hip.

He knew he'd really put his foot in it. "Uh…" he scrambled around in a brain, "…a woman?"

She wasn't buying it for a second.

"You're…startling!" It probably wasn't the most tactful thing to say, but she was.

"Haven't been called that before."

"Well you damn well should have been!" And beautiful! Not like some magazine, but the woman fit what little he knew of her so perfectly that he realized she couldn't look any other way and still be herself.

Felisha's skin shone as dark as the finest tan and her shoulder-length curls were dyed peach gold. Her lean features offset dark eyes that dominated her face. Her body was long and lean, but the strength she'd effortlessly demonstrated on the flight line showed as well.

Her smile was even better than her laugh. "A sweet Yankee? Who'da thought there ever was such a thing on God's ice-white Earth."

The rest of the day, evening, whatever it was under the land of the midnight sun, he'd spent tagging along with her. They'd checked in on the power plant where three massive diesel engines burned the jet fuel to spin electricity generators. Highly efficient exchangers captured all the waste heat from the engines, and heated up a glycol solution that was pumped throughout the station, warming the hydroponics room, and even drying clothes.

Over dinner, he ignored his crewmates and sat with Felisha, her crew, and Hubert the astrophysicist from the first day along with his own team. There was no line that he could detect between the support teams and the "beakers" or himself. They were a community at a hardship post that they hadn't simply chosen, but spent years vying for.

But did Felisha still want it?

It was hard to tell.

She knew the place better than he knew his parents' backyard, but he couldn't say if it fit her, either.

The only thing she griped about was the lack of peaches. Other than that, she was a magnet of positivity that drew others to her.

Did she *belong* here?

He didn't think so.

Felisha belonged…

In the summer sunshine. And an Antarctic one.

That sunlit night, she had one more surprise for him. With just a look, without a single word, she "asked" if he wanted to spend the night with her.

He'd used just as few words to say yes.

By halfway through the night he hoped that the storm over McMurdo never broke.

## 9
-----

FELISHA'S TEAM WORKED WITH STEVE FOR HOURS THE next morning re-warming the plane. Sitting for twenty-four hours at below minus forty, it had turned into a giant block of ice. At McMurdo, the temperature was hovering around freezing this time of year so they wouldn't have this problem. Here, even the cold-rated AN-8 fuel became sluggish, greased bearings might as well be frozen, and hydraulic oil was little better than glue.

They had to trundle out the forced-air heaters and ducting. One for each of the four engines and several more for the airplane's interior. And they couldn't do it fast unless they wanted to break things. Sudden and uneven heating could crack metal, even shatter windshields.

And through it all, she couldn't seem to stop smiling behind her peach scarf. Sure, what happened on The Ice stayed on The Ice, but living here long term and being one of the few women had made it very awkward—thirty-six guys and three women had overwintered. Sleep with two and you got "a reputation." Have a bad breakup with one, and it was a path to hell with nowhere to get away. She'd kept her few dalliances restricted to summer folk, and even among them there was a thing about bedding an "overwinter"—as if she was other than human.

Steve hadn't been some summer whim after a long, lonely winter. He'd found a way past her defenses so easily that she'd have scoffed if someone had warned her beforehand. And last night had simply been off the charts wonderful. Sleep deprivation was a real problem in the summer due to the sun never setting, but she didn't regret a single moment of not sleeping last night.

However, the McMurdo storm had been short and sharp, clearing off as quickly as it had arrived, so he was headed aloft.

When they were finally ready and had safely started the engines, her team quickly extracted all of the equipment.

"Next time, Brick."

"Next time, Felisha," he responded with a cheery wave. She didn't need to see his smile to feel it—his voice was so thick with it that it warmed her right through.

Then, like a total sap of a schoolgirl, she stayed out

in the cold and watched the plane as the four big engines roared to full power. The plane seemed to lean forward...but it didn't move an inch.

"Maybe it doesn't want to leave," Lamar shouted from close beside her as he collapsed the last of the heater ducting.

"Frozen skis." It was Lamar's first winterover and he'd arrived at the end of the summer, so he wouldn't have seen it before.

But the pilot knew what to do.

He eased off the engines, then hit the hydraulics to lower the wheels. They pushed down through the center of the skis and drove against the ice. He cycled them three times up and down, fully breaking the skis free. But she could see the bottoms of the skis were still caked with ice that had bonded harder to the steel than the other ice.

"Watch this. This is fun," she told Lamar before he could turn away thinking the show was over.

The plane lumbered and strained along the short taxiway and out onto the skiway. With the engines at full roar, it eased forward, still scraping at the rough ice frozen to the underside of the skis.

"Now!" she shouted to Lamar.

On cue, the eight rocket motors mounted along the sides of the fuselage fired, flaming back and down.

A hundred and fifty thousand pounds of loaded LC-130H lurched forward. In the fourteen seconds that the rockets burned, the plane slashed down the runway. Just at burnout, it rotated aloft.

With a waggle of wings it faded into the distance and was gone.

But Felisha felt she could wrap those simple words around herself and be content for many nights to come.

"Next time, Brick," she whispered to the empty blue sky.

# 10

---

ALL SUMMER, STEVE COUNTED THE HOURS UNTIL THERE
was another lift into the South Pole. The week that
their plane was down at McMurdo waiting for a part
would have been completely agonizing. Except his
captain had released him once the part was scheduled,
so he'd caught a lift to the Pole for three days.

Another time, he'd had forty-eight hours down as a
designated rest period. He'd deadheaded down on
another bird that morning and back the next.

That night they'd curled up in her bunk and
watched *Galaxy Quest*. After that, he started his own
little campaign to make the "*Never give up. Never
surrender.*" chest-thumping salute the unofficial one for
the 109th Airlift Wing.

But when they began ferrying more people out
than they were ferrying in Steve began to worry.

The South Pole had run with a hundred and fifty

people for almost three months, but now they were hauling them out in tens and twenties as the polar winter approached.

His time with Felisha, other than at the fuel pumps, was mostly stolen minutes. Yet by the beginning of February, there was no woman he knew as well. No woman he'd ever wanted to get to know better.

"It's our second-to-last run," he tried to keep his voice light. The sun, which had peaked at two handspans into the sky—a full twenty degrees—was now slipping along only a few finger-widths above the horizon, just as when they'd first met. The temperatures were falling, and Felisha was back to wearing her thick woolen peach scarf.

"Next week?" Her distress was obvious and he hated hearing it. Feeling it. Imagining her locked away in a South Polar winter for another nine months was just...wrong.

He nodded. "I wish to God you were coming with me. I'll be in Christchurch, New Zealand, next Friday. New York by Monday, just in time for spring."

She walked away along the fuel line, inspecting each connection for leaks. He'd learned to not get aggravated when she did things like that in the middle of a conversation, even when there wasn't a hose to inspect. He now knew that it was just what she did when she needed to think.

She was a long time coming back. When she did, she stopped close in front of him.

"I haven't seen spring in a long time."

"A New York one is amazing. Mom's garden wakes up in April and goes totally nuts in May. Rhododendrons kick in along with azaleas—you've never seen better colors than those two together. The oaks, maples, and birch go from bare sticks to so thick with green leaves that you wonder how they could be any other way, just holding up the blue sky."

He felt a little foolish but she made it okay by sliding the conversation sideways. She asked about the Air National Guard and the 109th Airlift Wing. About his plans to stay there. About his family, though he'd thought he'd told her everything about them over the summer. She asked more questions and seemed to simply enjoy listening to him retell stories of them.

## 11

Today was Last Flight.

For the next nine months, the South Pole Station would be physically cut off from the world, more remote and much harder to reach than even the International Space Station.

Felisha tried to remember the last time she'd been so nervous about something.

Her first time on The Ice? Watching the last flight depart before her first winterover at McMurdo? Standing at Mama's grave and wondering how her life could possibly go on?

She'd spent these last hours pacing, since the moment Steve's final trip had departed McMurdo three hours ago. She'd stood for an hour out in the minus-fifty cold staring at her name on this year's geographical pole marker.

The round brass disc of the horizon, a slice of

constellation-thick sky and another of brass-bright sun, all crossed with a band showing an outline of the South Pole Station itself. And on the vertical shaft below—square this year instead of round—her engraved name.

Last month, Steve had switched with one of the other crews and been here for the unveiling. He'd held her hand through their thick gloves during the brief ceremony—which was held at local midnight, of course.

Afterward, once the small crowd had dispersed back to their tasks or gone inside to celebrate the New Year, he'd stepped up to it and brushed a gloved fingertip over her name.

"Felisha Cole. At least now I know your last name." As if it hadn't been equally prominent on last year's marker.

He could make her laugh like no one had in years.

And now, at the last flight at the end of summer, she stood in the same place she had at the beginning of the summer, awaiting that first flight. Same spot. Southernmost end of the Jack F. Paulus Skiway.

The black dot—she spotted it first this time.

Its growth to a dot with a line of wing, then a plane, then a majestic LC-130H seemed to happen between one heartbeat and the next, yet to also take a thousand.

She waited until Steve was on the ice. Until the hose was connected and the fuel was transferring.

Waited until it was done, the hose was disconnected, and the others had driven off to the fuel arch.

He hugged her on his arrival, but had apparently been at a loss for further words—just as she was throughout the entire process.

Once it was just them, she fished two pieces of paper from her pocket and held them out to him. They crinkled and snapped in the bitter fall wind rushing out of the Clean Sector; she almost lost them downwind before Steve saved them from her numb fingers.

He read the first one quickly, glanced up at her as if to ask if she was sure.

How could she be?

He read the second one, starting fast, ending slow. Then he reread it.

She couldn't see his face when he finally looked up. She didn't need to as he crushed her to his chest. She buried her face against his shoulder. Now she could be sure.

The first was her resignation from the US Antarctic Program.

Lamar had been more than ready to take over as lead fuelie and all of her other roles here. Their summer assistant had almost died on the spot with joy at the last-minute chance to winterover.

And the second—

"The New York Air National Guard is going to *love* you!" Steve roared out, loud enough to hurt her ears despite their heavy hoods. His squeal of joy was simultaneously the best and the most ridiculous thing she'd ever heard.

The recruiter had offered her post of choice, and she'd asked for the 109th Airlift Wing. With her Antarctic experience, he'd signed her as fast as he could.

"And what about you, Brick?" Because that was the real question.

"Me? Are you kidding me, Felisha? I was gone on you long before you pulled back your hood that first time."

"Just like a Yankee, you can't say the words can you?"

"Don't have to, I've got something better. Where's your gear?"

She pointed at the two bags sitting on the ice next to where the snowcat had been parked.

Steve practically sprinted over to fetch them, as if she might change her mind if he wasn't quick enough.

He shooed her up onto the rear loading ramp.

The moment her feet left the ice she felt strangely dizzy, as if she wasn't connected to anything anymore.

"Something better than saying you love me?" She hadn't meant to sound needy, but it came out that way.

"Yep!"

"Aggravating man."

He ignored her mutter. "But I didn't want to push

until you'd chosen whether or not you were ready to leave The Ice."

"And what's this thing that's better than saying three goddamn words?"

"One word. Peaches."

"What?"

"The fifty miles of farmland from the 109th's base at Schenectady, New York, to my parents' place in Wheelerville grows the best peaches you ever tasted. Serve 'em up with the neighbor's cream practically fresh off the cow and I'll put them up against a Georgia peach any day!"

Felisha sputtered somewhere between a laugh and yelp before she found her voice. "Sweet Jesus! Why in the name of all that's holy didn't you say that before?"

"I wanted to make sure you didn't love me just for my peaches."

Felisha's laugh filled the crowded LC-130H's cargo bay as it prepared to head north for the winter. She'd be back on The Ice for the summers with the 109th, but she'd also have a home, a *life* with the best man she'd ever met.

And, goddamn it, she'd have peaches.

# DRONE (EXCERPT)

IF YOU ENJOYED THAT, YOU'LL LOVE
MIRANDA CHASE!

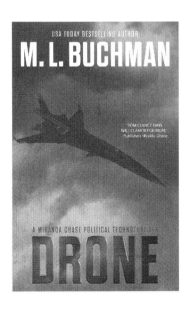

# DRONE (EXCERPT)

Flight 630 at 37,000 feet
12 nautical miles north of
Santa Fe, New Mexico, USA

THE FLIGHT ATTENDANT STEPPED UP TO HER SEAT—4E—
which had never been her favorite on a 767-300. At
least the cabin setup was in the familiar 261-seat, 2-
class configuration, currently running at a seventy-
three percent load capacity with a standard crew of ten
and one ride-along FAA inspector in the cockpit jump
seat.

"Excuse me, are you Miranda Chase?"

She nodded.

The attendant made a face that she couldn't
interpret.

A frown? Did that indicate anger?

He turned away before she could consider the possibilities and, without another word, returned to his station at the front of the cabin.

Miranda once again straightened the emergency exit plan that the flight's vibrations kept shifting askew in its pocket.

This flight from yesterday's meeting at LAX to today's DC lunch meeting at the National Transportation Safety Board's headquarters departed so early that she'd decided to spend the night in the airline's executive lounge working on various aviation accident reports. She never slept on a flight and would have to catch up on her sleep tonight.

Miranda felt the shift as the plane turned into a modest five-degree bank to the left. The bright rays of dawn over the New Mexico desert shifted from the left-hand windows to the right side.

At due north, she heard the Rolls-Royce RB211 engines (quite a pleasant high tone compared to the Pratt & Whitney PW4000 that she always found unnerving) ease off ever so slightly, signaling a slow descent. The pilot was transitioning from an eastbound course that would be flown at an odd number of thousands of feet to a westbound one that must be flown at an even number.

The flight attendant then picked up the intercom phone and a loud squawk sounded through the cabin. Most people would be asleep and there were soft complaints and rustling down the length of the aircraft.

"We regret to inform you that there is an emergency on the ground. I repeat, there is nothing wrong with the plane. We are being routed back to Las Vegas, where we will disembark one passenger, refuel, and then continue our flight to DC. Our apologies for the inconvenience."

There were now shouts of complaint all up and down the aisle.

The flight attendant was staring straight at her as he slammed the intercom back into its cradle with significantly greater force than was required to seat it properly.

Oh. It was her they would be disembarking. That meant there was a crash in need of an NTSB investigator—a major one if they were flying back an hour in the wrong direction.

Thankfully, she always had her site kit with her.

For some reason, her seatmate was muttering something foul. Miranda ignored it and began to prepare herself.

Only the crash mattered.

She straightened the exit plan once more. It had shifted the other way with the changing harmonic from the RB2II engines.

———

## Chengdu, Central China

AIR FORCE MAJOR WANG FAN EASED BACK ON THE joystick of the final prototype Shenyang J-31 jet—designed exclusively for the People's Liberation Army Air Force. In response, China's newest fighter jet leapt upward like a catapult's missile from the PLAAF base in the flatlands surrounding the towering city of Chengdu.

It felt as he'd just been grasped by Chen Mei-Li. Never had a woman made him feel like such a man.

———

*Get* Drone *and fly into a whole series of action and danger! Available at fine retailers everywhere.*
*Drone*

# ABOUT THE AUTHOR

USA Today and Amazon #1 Bestseller M. L. "Matt" Buchman started writing on a flight south from Japan to ride his bicycle across the Australian Outback. Just part of a solo around-the-world trip that ultimately launched his writing career.

From the very beginning, his powerful female heroines insisted on putting character first, *then* a great adventure. He's since written over 60 action-adventure thrillers and military romantic suspense novels. And just for the fun of it: 100 short stories, and a fast-growing pile of read-by-author audiobooks.

Booklist says: "3X Top 10 of the Year." PW says: "Tom Clancy fans open to a strong female lead will clamor for more." His fans say: "I want more now...of everything." That his characters are even more insistent than his fans is a hoot.

As a 30-year project manager with a geophysics degree who has designed and built houses, flown and jumped out of planes, and solo-sailed a 50' ketch, he is awed by what is possible. More at: www. mlbuchman.com.

# Other works by M. L. Buchman: *(* - also in audio)*

# Other works by M. L. Buchman:

## Contemporary Romance (cont)

### Love Abroad
*Heart of the Cotswolds: England*
*Path of Love: Cinque Terre, Italy*

### Where Dreams
*Where Dreams are Born*
*Where Dreams Reside*
*Where Dreams Are of Christmas**
*Where Dreams Unfold*
*Where Dreams Are Written*

## Science Fiction / Fantasy

### Deities Anonymous
*Cookbook from Hell: Reheated*
*Saviors 101*

### Single Titles
*The Nara Reaction*
*Monk's Maze*
*the Me and Elsie Chronicles*

## Non-Fiction

### Strategies for Success
*Managing Your Inner Artist/Writer*
*Estate Planning for Authors**
*Character Voice*
*Narrate and Record Your Own*
*Audiobook**

# Short Story Series by M. L. Buchman:

## Romantic Suspense

### Delta Force
*Th Delta Force Shooters*
*The Delta Force Warriors*

### Firehawks
*The Firehawks Lookouts*
*The Firehawks Hotshots*
*The Firebirds*

### The Night Stalkers
*The Night Stalkers 5D Stories*
*The Night Stalkers 5E Stories*
*The Night Stalkers CSAR*
*The Night Stalkers Wedding Stories*

### US Coast Guard

### White House Protection Force

## Contemporary Romance

### Eagle Cove

### Henderson's Ranch*

### Where Dreams

## Action-Adventure Thrillers

### Dead Chef

### Miranda Chase Origin Stories

## Science Fiction / Fantasy

### Deities Anonymous

### Other
*The Future Night Stalkers*
*Single Titles*

# SIGN UP FOR M. L. BUCHMAN'S NEWSLETTER TODAY

*and receive:*
*Release News*
*Free Short Stories*
*a Free Book*

*Get your free book today. Do it now.*
*free-book.mlbuchman.com*

Printed in Great Britain
by Amazon

62679860R00050